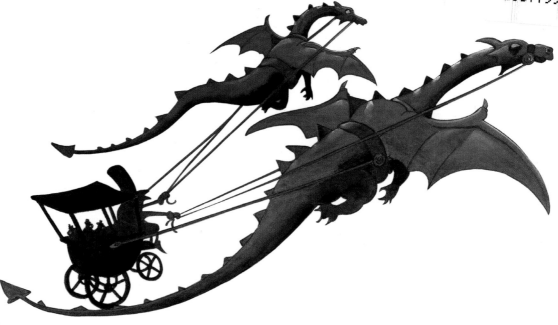

Engelbert Sneem

and his
Dream Vacuum Cleaner

Written & illustrated by

Mr Daniel Postgate

meadowside
CHILDREN'S BOOKS

In this world,
where we live,

it is really quite sad
That a number of people
grow up to be bad.

We have rascals and robbers
and cheaters and pinchers
And fibbers and squealers
and rotters and stinkers.
But out of them all
there is nobody meaner
Than Engelbert Sneem
and his Dream Vacuum Cleaner.

At night time, when children
slip into their beds
And onto soft pillows
they lay their sweet heads,
It isn't too long
before dreaming begins,
And while they are dreaming
of wonderful things…
Of fairies and flowers
and rainbows and kings.

From out of the darkness,

out of the gloom,
Mr Engelbert Sneem
tip-toes into the room

And he sucks up their dreams
with his dreadful machine
Then leaps out the window
before he is seen.

He puts all the dreams
into pottery flagons,
Climbs on his carriage
and screams to his dragons,
*"Come open your wings,
pretty lizards, take flight!"*
Then Engelbert Sneem
flies away through the night.

To a Kingdom of permanent
darkness he flies
Where a restless and rampaging
storm fills the skies.
Where rumbling thunder
and lightening flashes
Across a dark sea
which perpetually crashes
Against a black rock,
on which stands at its peak,

The Castle of Sneem,

oh so silent and bleak.

Down echoing stairs goes the burgling rascal,
Dragging his sack to the bowels of his castle
Where flagons are stored upon old wooden beams...

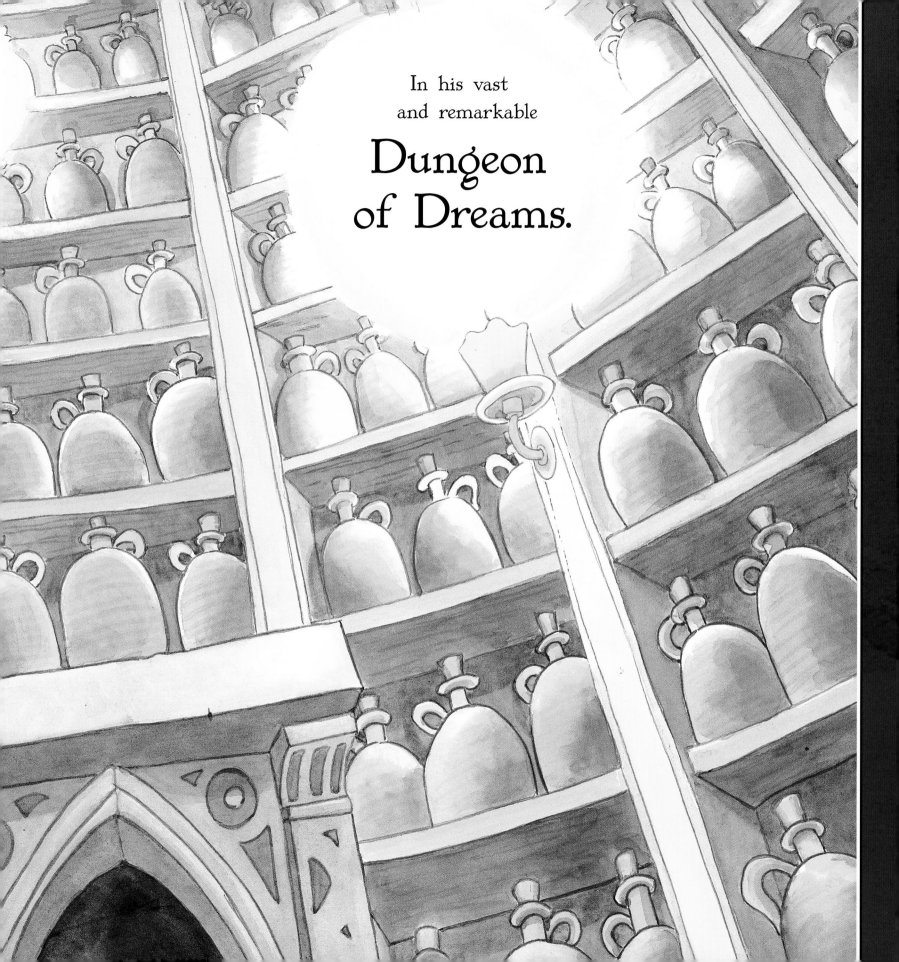

In his vast
and remarkable

Dungeon
of Dreams.

Then if ever Sneem
fancies a nice little treat,
He picks out a flagon
that's cheeky and sweet,
He pops out the cork
with the greatest of pleasure,
Then savours a sumptuous
dream at his leisure.

And I very much doubt
whether Sneem's ever wondered
What happens to children
whose dreams he has plundered.
Why, robbed of their dreaming
they grow up to be
Those miserable adults
you so often see.

A little boy said to his mum,
"Is this right?
Is there really a man
who steals dreams every night?"
"Oh, hush now my child,"
said his mum, "take a look!
It is only a tale
in a fairy tale book.

"You sleep now my darling
and have a nice dream."
And he did have a dream,
but the dream was of Sneem.

And while the boy dreamt
of the tale he had read,
A shadowy figure crept up to his bed
And he sucked up the dream
and he plugged it up tight,
Then he chuckled and
scuttled away through the night.

Once back in his castle,
the crook, with great pleasure,
Pulled out the cork
from his freshly caught treasure.
And as the dream
billowed and swirled through the air,
A shocking and scandalous tale
was laid bare...

The tale of a greedy
and pilfering thief
Who left in his wake
only sadness and grief.
Cried Engelbert Sneem
(for of course it was he)...

In absolute horror
  Sneem let out such screams
That they shattered the thousands
  of flagons of dreams.
And all of those wonderful dreams,
  they took flight,
Transforming the darkness
  to sweetness and light.
The sea became calm
  and the sky became blue,
Then up and away
  those most splendid dreams flew...

  Back to the people
  to whom they belong,
  Bringing them happiness,

    laughter

    and song.

Alone, in his throne room,
Sneem pondered his plight
(With just an umbrella
to keep off the light).
He sat and he brooded
for days upon days,
Then finally whispered,

"I must change my ways."

And now...
if a child
has frightening dreams
Of ghosties and ghoulies
and terrible things.

The good Mr Sneem
is right there in a tick,
And he sucks up the nightmare
and plugs it up quick.
Then he carefully writes
on the flagon with chalk:

'Please
leave this alone,

Never pull
out the cork!'

And he takes it away
to his dungeon...
so then...

That child will never
have nightmares again.

For Harry

This edition published in 2007
by Meadowside Children's Books
185 Fleet Street, London, EC4A 2HS
Text and illustrations
© Daniel Postgate 2006

The right of Daniel Postgate to be identified
as the author and illustrator of this work
has been asserted by him in accordance with the
Copyright, Designs and Patents Act, 1988

A CIP catalogue record for this book
is available from the British Library
Printed in China
10 9 8 7 6 5 4 3 2 1